Einstein Anderson
science geek

The Mighty Ants
and Other Cases

Seymour Simon
Illustrations by Kevin O'Malley

SCHOLASTIC INC.

Text copyright © 2014 by Seymour Simon.
Illustrations copyright © 2014 by Kevin O'Malley.
All rights reserved. Published by Scholastic Inc., 557 Broadway, New York, NY 10012, by arrangement with StarWalk Kids Media.
Printed in the U.S.A.

ISBN-13: 978-1-338-05342-5
ISBN-10: 1-338-05342-6

SCHOLASTIC and associated logos are trademarks and/or registered trademarks of Scholastic Inc.

1 2 3 4 5 6 7 8 9 10   40   25 24 23 22 21 20 19 18 17 16

Contents

Camera in a Cage

Einstein Anderson looked out across a plain in Kenya.

Well, not exactly. He was looking out on a large animal enclosure at the Daniels County Zoo. An elephant stood nearby. Scattered across a large field were small groups of zebras and antelopes. A pride of lions—one large male, several females, and their young cubs—lazed about in the shade of a clump of trees. Of course, they were separated from the elephant, zebras, and antelopes by a wide moat.

"Hold still, *Einstein!*" Paloma Fuentes told him as he held up her phone to take a photo. "I want to get a picture of you on a safari."

Einstein pushed his tortoise-shell glasses back onto the bridge of his nose and tried to smile for the camera. He was used to people teasing him about his nickname, especially Paloma.

Albert Einstein was one of the most brilliant scientists who ever lived, someone who discovered many important things about the nature of matter and the universe. His equation $E=MC^2$ led to the understanding of atomic energy.

Einstein Anderson was just a normal-looking twelve-year-old with brown hair who liked to wear old, torn jeans and T-shirts. His real name was Adam but ever since kindergarten people had been calling him Einstein, because he seemed to know more about science than anyone else. He had a reputation for solving mysteries and everyday problems by using science.

But Einstein Anderson was also a sixth grader at Sparta Middle School and today he was on a trip with Ms. Taylor's science class.

"Move a little to the left," Paloma was saying. She waved her hand to point and her long, black ponytail shook. She was dressed as though she was going on a safari, in tan hiking shorts and a shirt with big pockets. (Although, as usual, she wore red canvas high tops on her feet.)

She peered at the camera screen. "Look like you're really in Africa," she instructed.

Einstein had no idea how he would do that, but he didn't argue. Paloma had strong opinions and sometimes it was better to just ignore them. She was also Einstein's best friend, and had been for a few years. She was the only person he knew who cared about science as much as he did.

"Move a little more," she said. "Now look at the lions, and . . ." she stopped and frowned. "Pat, you get in the picture, too."

"Me?"

Pat Hong was just a few feet away. He was a tall kid, who looked like the athlete he was. His straight black hair was cut short and he usually wore his Sparta soccer team jersey. Pat and Einstein had become friends the previous summer. He coached Einstein in his soccer game and Einstein helped him with his science homework.

Pat also got strangely tongue-tied whenever

he was around Paloma. Everyone noticed this except her.

"Just stand next to Einstein," Paloma was saying, as she peered at the phone's screen. "No, not like that."

Pat didn't say anything. He just looked at Einstein for help. But Einstein could only shrug. "Look like you're in Africa," he advised. "Hey, that reminds me, why did the lion always lose at cards?"

"Oh, please!" Paloma protested. Einstein was also famous for jokes and puns. Once he started, it was very hard to stop him.

"Because," Einstein said, with a big laugh, "he was playing with a cheetah!"

"That was bad, Einstein," Pat told him.

Their teacher, Ms. Taylor, came around the corner of a building, leading a bunch of kids from their class.

"Now, here is the African Plains exhibit," she was telling them. "You can see the African elephant here is different from the Asian elephant. African elephants grow to be taller, with bigger ears, and are a little swaybacked. If you haven't already, please fill out your trip-sheets with your observations."

The group stopped and Ms. Taylor called out to Einstein and his friends.

"Paloma, Pat, and Adam," she said. "I assume you've already finished your assignments." For some reason Ms. Taylor refused to call Einstein by his nickname. Einstein thought it was because she didn't think she could teach someone named Einstein.

"Yes, Ms. Taylor," Paloma answered.

"Well, have fun exploring, but please be back at the snack bar by twelve."

"Yes, Ms. Taylor," Paloma said again. Then

she turned to Pat and Einstein. "Come on, I want to see the giraffes." Without waiting for an answer, she began walking toward the giraffe enclosure.

"Hey, wait up!" someone called out. It was Jamal Henry, another kid in their class. He broke off from Ms. Taylor's group and came running after them.

"Man, look at those necks," he said as they followed the steel fence around the exhibit. "They must be ten feet long."

"More like six or seven feet," Paloma told him. "A male giraffe's head can be 18 feet off the ground because their legs are very long too. A giraffe neck weighs about 600 pounds."

"Gee!" Pat said. Einstein knew that Pat was impressed by Paloma's knowledge of giraffes, but unfortunately it came out as a sort of squeak. Pat's face turned red.

"Hey," Einstein said quickly. "Guess how many bones there are in a giraffe's neck?"

"Is this some kind of corny joke?" Paloma asked.

"No," Einstein replied. "But it could be, if you want."

"No, no," Paloma said, laughing. "One is enough. Well, if it's not a joke, the answer is seven, the same number as in a mouse or a dog or a human being."

"Hmm, that is very interesting," Pat said, speaking in the lowest voice he could manage.

"And they don't have vocal chords," Jamal added.

"A lot of people believe that, but actually giraffes do have vocal chords," Paloma replied. "Sorry, I just happen to like giraffes. That's why I know so much ab . . . what is going on there?"

The four kids stopped in their tracks. There

was a small crowd of about a dozen people gathered by the giraffe enclosure. Behind the black metal railing there was a drop of about ten feet into a kind of moat filled with low bushes. The moat and bushes kept the giraffes from getting too close to the people, and vice versa.

A couple of the zookeepers, dressed in their green zoo uniforms, were at the railing, trying to hold the crowd back. Meanwhile, a third zookeeper was below, in the enclosure with the giraffes, on her hands and knees. She was clearly looking for something in the moat.

"Maybe someone fell in," Jamal said.

"Maybe the giraffe is sick," Paloma replied, sounding worried.

"Let's go find out," said Einstein.

The four of them hurried over.

As they got closer they could see that in the

middle of the crowd was a young woman who was talking to one of the zookeepers. She was short with curly black hair and was wearing jeans, brown leather sandals, and a green top. On her shoulder was a large canvas bag. Einstein thought she looked like a college student. She looked pretty upset.

"I have to get that camera back," she was saying as they got closer. "I borrowed it from my friend. I don't know how I can afford to replace it."

One of the zookeepers, a tall man with a big bushy mustache, was trying to reassure her.

"If it fell in the enclosure, we'll find it," he said, calmly. "You did the right thing by calling us instead of trying to get it yourself."

"But what if it broke?" the young woman went on. "What if it hit a rock?"

"Let's just see," the man replied reassuringly.

Just then there was a shout from below. "Got it!"

A few people applauded.

"Way to go, zookeepers," Jamal said, as he clapped, also.

"I hope her camera is okay," said Einstein.

"I hope the giraffe wasn't hurt," added Paloma.

Less than a minute later the woman zoo-keeper from inside the enclosure appeared on the sidewalk, carrying a video camera.

"You're lucky," she said. "It fell on a bush. I don't think it's damaged."

The young woman's face brightened as she reached for the video camera.

"Oh, thank you," she cried. "That is so great!"

"Hold on!" someone yelled. A middle-aged woman pushed her way through the small crowd. She was slim and her blond hair was cut short in a very stylish way. She was dressed all in black—black pants, black T-shirt, black shoes, and a black leather shoulder bag.

"Wait a minute," she said, as she walked up to the woman zookeeper. "That's my camera!"

There was a buzz from the crowd.

"Uh-oh," Paloma muttered. Einstein nodded.

"Double uh-oh," said Jamal.

"What do you mean?" protested the younger woman, who still had her hands out, reaching for the camera. "I dropped it over the fence by accident."

"No, I dropped it!" the older woman replied with an icy tone. "I've been looking all over for the zookeepers to help me get it out." She turned to the woman zookeeper and said with a big smile, "I'll take it now, thank you."

13

The woman zookeeper with the camera hesitated. She looked to the other zookeepers. The one with the mustache cleared his throat.

"Do you have any proof that this is your camera?" he asked the younger woman.

"No," she said, getting upset again. "I told you, I borrowed it. I was taping the giraffes and I lost my grip and it fell in, just like I told you."

The zookeeper turned to the blond woman who was dressed in black. "What about you?" he asked. "Do you have any proof?"

The blond woman shook her head angrily. "No," she replied. "Who carries proof around with them? I was filming here about fifteen minutes ago. There was no one else here and I leaned in to get a better angle when one of the giraffes screamed. It startled me so much I dropped the camera."

The two zookeepers looked at each other, then the man shrugged. "I guess we'll just have to take this to the administration office and let them sort it out," he said.

Just then Einstein spoke up. "I don't think you have to do that," he said. "One of these women is lying and I can prove it."

Can you solve the mystery? How does Einstein know which one of the stories is fake?

"**Hold on,**" the male zookeeper said. "It's pretty serious to call someone a liar."

"That's right, little boy," the blond woman added. "You should be more careful about throwing around charges like that."

"I *am* careful," Einstein replied very calmly. "And I'm one hundred percent certain that your story can't be true—because giraffes don't scream."

There was a nodding of heads in the crowd.

"He's right," the zookeeper said, turning to the blond woman. "I wasn't paying attention. Of course giraffes don't scream. You better get out of here before we call the police."

"Why . . . I . . ." the woman sputtered, but then she quickly turned and headed for the exit.

The second zookeeper handed the video camera to the young woman with the curly hair.

"Here you go," she said. "But be more careful next time."

"I will!" the young woman said, taking the camera. Then she turned to Einstein. "Thank you so much!" she cried, and then suddenly gave him a big hug. Einstein found himself being crushed against the video camera.

"Uh . . . thanks?" he mumbled when she let him go. He wasn't sure, but he thought now *his* face was turning red.

As the crowd broke up, Jamal turned to Einstein. "I don't get it," he asked. "How come giraffes can't scream? Paloma said they have vocal chords."

"They do," Paloma told him. "But they don't use them very much and they never scream."

"The loudest sound they make is a sort of low cough," Einstein added.

"Like this?" Pat asked and he made a coughing noise. At the sound, the giraffe turned its head and stared at Pat.

"Better watch out," Einstein replied, laughing. "Maybe that was a giraffe mating call! Which reminds me . . ."

"Uh-oh, again," said Jamal. But Einstein was already laughing at his own joke.

"Do you know why you can't tell who wins a giraffe race? Because it's always neck and neck!"

From: Einstein Anderson
To: Science Geeks
Experiment: The Ear of the Beholder

Hi Geeks:

Did you ever notice that people have a tendency to exaggerate when they are lying? I mean, that woman might have gotten the camera if she hadn't added the screaming giraffe to her story. Geeks always pay attention to the details!

Here's a detail that might interest you: We think of giraffes as being silent animals, but actually they do make sounds. They cough and whistle to their mates and their young, and they've been known to communicate by moaning, snoring, hissing, and making sounds like a flute. In fact, the giraffe has quite a vocabulary! But the main way giraffes communicate is by *infrasonic* sound. Infrasonic sounds are very low pitch, under 18 Hz (that's short for "hertz," and it's the unit of measurement for the pitch of sounds. The loudness of a sound is measured in *decibels*.) The human ear can only hear sounds from about 20 Hz at the low end up to about 20 kHz (the k stands for one thousand, so you could write 20 kHz as 20,000 Hz). Giraffes may be talking all the time; we just can't hear them!

While we are on the subject of sounds and hearing, I bet you are wondering how you hear what you do hear. Let's do an experiment and find out.

Here is what you need:

• Plastic wrap
• String or a strong rubber band
• A jar or bowl with a wide opening
• Uncooked rice (or any other small grain)
• A metal pot or cookie sheet
• A spoon

Put the plastic wrap over the top of the jar or bowl and tie the string or rubber band around the rim to make sure it won't come loose. Put a few grains of rice on top of the plastic wrap. Pick up the pot or cookie sheet and hit it with the spoon. Really go to town, making the loudest noise you can. What happens? See those grains jumping around on the plastic? What's going on?

The Science Solution

When you made that noise, the sound traveled in waves from the pan. When the sound waves hit the plastic wrap, they made it vibrate, which made the rice jump. When sound waves reach your ear, they make the eardrum vibrate in a similar way—the higher the pitch, the faster the vibration.

By the way, kids can hear much higher-pitched sounds than adults. As we get older, eardrums get less flexible so they don't vibrate as fast. You probably know that dogs can hear higher pitched sounds than people, but cats can hear much higher pitches than people *or* dogs. Also, cats have 20 muscles to move their ears around and sense very accurately what direction a sound is coming from, while humans have only 6 ear-moving muscles, which aren't good for much except making people laugh. Can you wiggle your ears? Give it a try!

The Mighty Ants

"**This is more** than just a pet, *Einstein*," said Stanley Roberts. "This is going to create a whole new economy and StanTastic Industries will be at the center of it!"

"Oh, come on, Stanley," replied Paloma, shaking her head and frowning. Her long, black ponytail swayed back and forth. "This is another of your crazy schemes."

Einstein Anderson pushed his glasses back

onto the bridge of his nose and looked from Paloma to Stanley, then sighed. Paloma was right, this did seem like another crazy scheme.

He and Paloma and Stanley were standing in Sparta Pet Shack, a large pet store right in the middle of town. The aisles of the store were lined with brightly lit fish tanks, bird cages with colorful birds, and more tanks with all sorts of small animals. But Einstein and his friends were looking at a display of ant farm kits.

"I don't care what you say, *Einstein*," Stanley said, mockingly. "You think you're such a genius, but this time, you're wrong."

Stanley was in Einstein and Paloma's class at Sparta Middle School. He thought he knew a lot about science, too. Unfortunately, he never bothered to read much about science or even watch a show on the Science Channel. Stanley's big dream was to invent some new kind of technology and become a billionaire like Mark Zuckerberg or Steve Jobs. He'd even thought up his own corporation, StanTastic Industries.

Usually Stanley dressed the way he imagined the CEO of a big corporation would dress, in a suit jacket, a white shirt, and a red and blue striped tie. But today, to visit the pet store, he was dressed like Einstein, in blue jeans, T-shirt, and sneakers.

"Come on, Stanley," Paloma protested. "This is just like the time you bought a baby Loch Ness Monster. Remember that?"

Stanley looked a little embarrassed. It was true. Einstein and Paloma had proved that his baby "Loch Ness Monster" was really just a salamander.

"I knew it wasn't a Loch Ness Monster," he said, "I was just joking around. Anyway, this time is different."

Paloma frowned. "Yeah, right!" she muttered.

Paloma was almost always right, but sometimes Einstein thought she was a little too quick to tell people they were wrong. Like now.

"Stanley, what are you going to do with all these ants?" she said, sounding annoyed. "Train them to do tricks?"

"Do you think I'm nuts?" Stanley quipped. Then, before Paloma could reply, he added dramatically. "I'm going to create a breed of giant ants. We'll be able to harness them to do work. Think of all the energy we'll save! And all the money I'll make."

Paloma turned to Stanley. "What are you talking about?" she asked. "What will you do with giant ants?"

"An ant can carry many times its own weight. It can climb straight up a wall. It can fall from

a tall building and not get hurt," Stanley recited this like he'd practiced it many times.

He took out his phone. "Look," he said excitedly, and held up the screen. On it was a photo of a very large ant. "This is the bulldog ant from Australia. It grows to be an inch and a half long. Just think if it was the size of a real bulldog! Why, it would be super strong."

"Like Spiderman," Paloma said, giggling. "Except this would be Antman."

"Hey, that reminds me," Einstein said. Paloma and Stanley both turned to him at the same time. They knew that Einstein had the habit of making up puns and silly jokes.

"Not now, Einstein," they said, together.

"Well, at least I got you two to agree on something," he said. "But what I was going to say was, Stanley could call his giant ants eleph-ants!"

"Hey, that's not a bad idea!" Stanley said. "Uh, do you mind if I use it?"

"This *is* nuts," Paloma objected. "How are you going to train ants to get together and carry heavy objects?"

"Well, ants already work together," Einstein pointed out. "They do it naturally."

"See?" Stanley said. "They do it naturally!"

"And it *is* true that ants are very strong for their size," Einstein added. "They can carry maybe twenty times their weight, or more. An Olympic weightlifter can only lift about five or six times his own weight. Of course an ant weighs almost nothing, a tiny fraction of an ounce—just a few milligrams—so carrying twenty times its weight isn't that much. "

"Yeah," Stanley nodded. "But twenty times their weight. Think about it."

"I don't have to think about it!" Paloma replied impatiently. "I know all about ants. Like they don't have bones like us. Their shells are their skeletons—exoskeletons. Their muscles are *inside* their skeletons. Plus, they have very thick muscles compared to their size."

"Yeah, that's what I said," Stanley told them. "But the main thing is how strong they are. Imagine how much stronger they will be if they are the size of a dog. Or a horse! If an ant was a hundred pounds, it could carry two thousand pounds or more."

"Well, okay. Forget about the strength for a minute," Paloma said impatiently. "How are you going to breed the ants and make them bigger?"

"The instructions come with the kit," Stanley said, pointing to the ant farms. "I'll start with small ants and then pick the biggest queens. It will take a while, but at the end I'll be famous—and rich!"

Just then, the clerk near the front of the store called out. He was a tall, thin high-school kid, who wore a plaid flannel shirt and dirty tan pants. His long brown hair was held back by a bandana.

"Hey, kid!" the clerk said. "Are you going to order those ant farms or not?"

"Ant *farms*?" Paloma repeated. "How many are you going to buy?"

"Two dozen," Stanley said calmly. "The more ants I raise, the more money I'll make."

"But how much will that cost?" Paloma asked.

"All my savings," Stanley replied. "But I'll make it all back in profit."

"I'm afraid not." Einstein sighed and shook his head. "Stanley, even if you could figure out how to breed giant ants, which I doubt, your scheme won't work. And I can prove it."

Can you solve the mystery? Why won't Stanley's scheme work?

"Oh, you're just jealous," Stanley huffed. "Because I thought of it and you didn't."

"Maybe you thought of it," Einstein told him, "but you didn't think of one important thing. An ant's muscles are relatively larger than bigger animals."

Stanley looked confused. "Relatively larger?" he said.

"That's what I've been trying to tell you," Einstein explained. "It has more muscle for its weight than bigger animals. Compared to the whole ant, ant muscle is very thick. So it's not hard for an ant to lift many times its weight. But an ant is very, very tiny."

"But if you made the ant bigger . . ." Stanley began.

"Its muscles would get bigger," Einstein said.

"But so would the rest of it," Paloma jumped in. "And—here's the important part, its overall size would get much bigger compared to its muscles. Its muscles would be small compared to the rest of it. If the ant was one hundred times stronger, it would be one thousand times heavier. It wouldn't even be able to move."

"That means it wouldn't be able to carry any-thing," said a disappointed Stanley.

"It wouldn't even be able to carry itself," Einstein said. "A gigantic ant would collapse under its own weight."

"Giant ants are just something you see in movies," Paloma told him. "They can't really exist."

"Hey, kid!" the clerk called out again. "What about it?"

Stanley shook his head. "Uh, no thanks," he said. "I just realized my calculations were incorrect." The clerk shrugged and went back to texting on his phone.

"Don't feel bad, Stanley," Einstein said, as the three of them left the store. "I have a better idea for you."

"You do?" Stanley said, brightening up.

"Sure," Einstein said with a serious look. "You could breed ants that had frog legs."

"Ants with frog legs?" Stanley replied, his eyes widening. "Is it possible?"

"Sure," Einstein told him. Then he started to laugh. "Haven't you ever heard of ant-phibeans?"

From: Einstein Anderson
To: Science Geeks
Experiment: Pets in a Jar

Hi Geeks:

Ants are small, but they are everywhere! About 12,400 different species of ants have been identified in the world today—and entomologists (scientists who study ants and other insects) believe there are over 20,000 species in all. Ants have adapted to many different climates. The Honey Pot Ant, which lives in dry desert areas of Australia, stores food and water in the abdomen of certain worker ants called "repletes." The repletes share their stored food in dry seasons.

Would you like to have your own ant colony to watch and observe?

Here is what you need to do:

Ants are social animals, which means they live in groups with others of their species. To survive, an ant family, or colony, as it's called, must have a queen. The ant queen is not ruler of the colony, but she is the one who lays eggs from which all the other ants develop. Usually, the queen is the founder of the colony. So if you want your colony to last, you must try to find a queen.

There is a day or two, usually in the summer, when winged ants are pushed outside their colony by the other ants. They try their wings for the first time and meet winged ants from other, nearby colonies. Most of these winged ants are male, but a few are female. You can tell the females because they are much larger than the males. During the swarm, the females mate and then they go off to start a new colony. The males live only a day or two before they die.

The queen begins by laying just a few eggs. They soon hatch and pass through the stages of metamorphosis, where they start as wormlike larvae, form a cocoon, and emerge as adult ants. The adult ants from the queen's first eggs are called "workers." They take on all the chores of the nest. They go out and find food for the queen and the other ants. They take care of the new eggs and the young that develop. They build tunnels, keep the nest clean, and defend it if necessary. Some species have a special kind of ant, called a soldier, with a large head and powerful jaws. Its job is defense.

Here is what you need to start an ant colony of your own:

- A large jar
- A chunk of wood that will fit in the jar
- Dirt
- Screen material or an old stocking
- Rubber bands
- Plastic bags (preferably zip-closing)
- Newspaper
- A shovel
- A large spoon

- Access to a refrigerator
- Dark construction paper
- Tape
- Water
- Bits of food—fruit, vegetables, meat, breadcrumbs, cereal, sugar water

Start by putting a block of wood in the center of the jar and packing dirt around it. This is so that the ants will build their tunnels near the outside of the jar where you will be able to see them. Make a cover out of fine mesh screening or an old stocking and hold it firmly in place with a rubber band so your pets don't invade your house.

Assuming it's not swarming season, look for ants under rocks or rotting logs. You may find common black ants in a nearby field or vacant lot. When you find an entrance to an ant colony, spread out newspaper on the ground nearby. Dig down in the soil with your shovel and put the loose dirt on the newspaper. Look for ants, small white ant eggs, larger cocoons, and small wriggling larvae. Use the spoon to put these into a plastic bag.

Look carefully for an ant that is much larger than the others. This is a queen. Sometimes a queen will crawl under the paper to hide. Be sure to lift up the newspaper and look. If you find a queen your colony will be able to last and grow.

Back home, put the plastic bag into the refrigerator (not the freezer!) for about an hour. Cold ants are sluggish and they'll be easier to transplant into their new home. The actual transfer is best done outside. Spread the contents of your plastic bag on some newspaper and, as quickly as you can, scoop them from there into the jar. Cover the jar right away so your new pets don't become unwelcome household guests.

It's a good idea to wrap some dark paper around the jar and hold it in place with a rubber band. This will encourage the ants to build tunnels near the glass when it is dark. Leave the jar alone for a few days so the ants can get used to their new home. They will do best at room temperature, not too close to direct sunlight or a radiator.

Keep the soil moist with a few drops of water. Don't let it get too wet or mold will form. After the first few days, feed the ants regularly. Try feeding them with bits of fruit, vegetables, bread, or cereal, or a few drops of sugar water. Use a small piece of paper as a feeding dish. Every two days, take out the paper and put in a new piece with some fresh food.

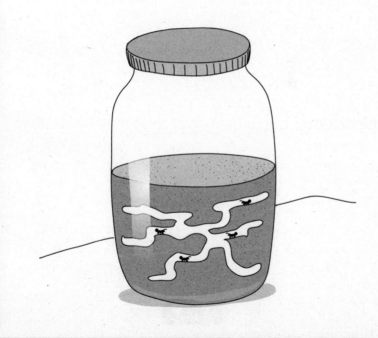

Now start keeping records of what you observe. What foods do your ants like best? Are they building tunnels? What do they do in the tunnels? How do they greet each other? Does the temperature or amount of light affect ant activities? Can you design an experiment to find out?

Have fun with your ant colony and remember—never give your uncle an anteater!

Star Wish

"Einstein, the moon is really bright. Did someone turn up the brightness level?"

Einstein looked at his little brother, Dennis, who was sitting next to him on their back porch. Dennis was eight, and unlike his big brother, he didn't seem interested in science. But Dennis had a way of asking weird questions that made Einstein think—like this one.

Einstein looked to his friend, Pat Hong, who was sitting in a wicker chair across from them.

"I don't know, Einstein," Pat said. "He's *your* brother."

It was a Friday evening in May, and thanks to daylight savings time, the sun was just going down at eight o'clock. Pat had come over for dinner with the Andersons and then three of them played catch in the backyard. But now it was almost too dark to see the ball.

"What do you mean, turn up the brightness?" Einstein asked Dennis, trying to choose his words carefully.

"I mean, they adjusted the settings to make it brighter," Dennis replied. Einstein couldn't be sure, but he though his little brother was serious.

"Dennis, you know that the sky is not a video screen, right?" he asked.

"Sure, I know that," Dennis replied in an injured voice. "What do you think I am, some dumb little kid?"

"But you said . . ." Einstein began, then took a deep breath. "When you look up in the sky at the moon, you're looking across space. You're looking directly at the moon. It's really up there."

"I didn't ask you if the moon was there," Dennis said, impatiently. "I can *see* it's there. I asked why it's so bright."

Pat laughed quietly. Einstein took another breath and started over.

"The moon doesn't have any light of its own," he explained. "Moonlight is reflected sunlight."

"Well, that doesn't make sense, Einstein," Dennis said confidently.

"Why not?"

"Because the moon shines at night when there's no sun."

Pat laughed again. "He's got you there, Einstein," he said.

"No, he doesn't!" Einstein replied. "Hold on a minute." He jumped up and went inside. His parents, Emily and Matt Anderson, were cleaning up from dinner.

"Mom, can I borrow your tablet?" Einstein asked. "I want to show Dennis something with the astronomy app."

"Of course, dear," his mother replied. "I'm so glad you and Dennis have something in common."

"Uh, yeah, sure," Einstein mumbled. He grabbed the tablet from the kitchen counter and went out the back door.

"Look," he said to Dennis and Pat, as he ran his finger over the touch screen. "Here's an animated view of the moon, the sun, and the earth. You can see it takes a little more than twenty-eight days for the moon to orbit the earth. The side of the moon facing the sun is always light, and the side that faces away is always dark."

"You're wrong again, *Einstein*," Dennis insisted. "Everyone knows the moon changes. Sometimes it's a circle and sometimes it's like a sideways smile and sometimes you can't see it at all."

Pat was trying not to laugh even harder.

"Yeah, *Einstein*," he said, teasingly. "How do you explain that?"

Einstein shook his head. Pat wasn't being any help at all.

"I explain it like this," he said, holding up the tablet. "See, the moon doesn't really change—what changes is the part that we see. As the moon moves around the earth we see it from different angles. Sometimes we just see the half that is in sunlight. That's the full moon. Sometimes we see part of the moon that is in sunlight and part that is in shadow. That's a half moon or a crescent moon. And then sometimes the side that is in shadow is toward us—we call that the new moon."

"Where do they get the new moon?" Dennis asked, innocently. Sometimes Einstein thought that Dennis got things mixed up on purpose just to annoy him.

"It's not really *new*," he explained, trying to stay patient. "It's just beginning the cycle again." He tried to change the subject.

"The moon reflects light," he said. "But stars make their own light."

"They do?" Dennis asked.

"Yes," Einstein replied, feeling pleased that Dennis was finally listening.

Dennis scratched his head, "Where do they get the electricity?"

"Just give up, Einstein," Pat laughed.

"They don't need electricity," Einstein said. "There's a nuclear reaction going on in the stars. That's what causes the light and heat."

"No, I don't think so," Dennis said, very seriously.

"Why not?" Einstein sighed.

"Well, you told me once that the sun is a star. Is that still true?"

"Yes, it's still true," Einstein told him. "It's been true for like, four and a half billion years."

"Well, then," Dennis said, calmly. "The sun is a star and it uses electricity. Haven't you ever heard of solar power?"

"Now I really give up!" Einstein said, beginning to laugh himself.

"Oh, look, a star!" Dennis cried.

The sun was almost below the horizon and a very bright light was shining not far from it in the sky.

"Star light, star bright," Dennis said. "First star I see tonight, wish I may and wish I might, have the wish I wish tonight."

"Sorry, Dennis," Pat said. "But you're not going to get your wish."

"Why not?" Dennis protested. "Who's going to stop me?"

"No one," Pat said. "It's just that you're not wishing on a star. Isn't that right, Einstein?"

"Well, yeah," Einstein nodded. "That's Venus. Although people sometimes call it the Evening Star."

"See!" Dennis cried. "The Evening Star! I get my wish!"

"Well, they *call* it the evening star," Einstein said, "but it's still a planet."

"Sorry, Dennis," Pat said. "Why don't you try wishing on a real star?"

"You only get one a night," Dennis complained. "Why'd you go and spoil it?"

"Well, you can't wish on a planet," Pat said.

"It's not a planet!" Dennis insisted.

"Hold on, Dennis," Einstein said. "I think there's a way you can both be right."

Can you solve the mystery? Why does Einstein say that Pat and Dennis can both be right?

"**Venus** is definitely a planet, not a star," Einstein continued.

"How do you know?" Dennis asked.

"Well, for one thing, stars are all over the sky," Einstein explained, "but planets always follow the same path as the sun. Second, planets are the brightest objects in the sky, after the sun and the moon."

"I didn't know that," Pat said.

"Yes, they're brighter than stars because planets are much, much closer to earth," Einstein told him. "And because they're closer and brighter, they don't usually twinkle the way stars do. But that's also why you're partly right, Dennis."

"Yeah?" Dennis asked. "How come?"

"Because planets, like the moon, don't have light of their own. They shine with reflected sunlight," Einstein said with a smile. "And, as you know, Dennis, the sun is . . ."

"A star!" Dennis shouted.

"That's right," Einstein said. "So you were wishing on a planet, but you were also wishing on . . ."

"Starlight reflected off of the planet, Venus! I knew it!" Dennis shouted. He pumped his fist in victory at Pat, who only laughed, good-naturedly.

"Hey," Einstein told him. "Why don't you go inside and ask Dad for the binoculars and we'll take a closer look at the moon. And by the way, do you know how you can tell when the moon is broke?"

"Uh-oh, here it comes," Pat winced.

"When it's down to its last quarter!" Einstein laughed at his own joke, but Dennis moaned unhappily.

"What's wrong?" Pat asked. "The joke wasn't that bad."

"That's not it," Dennis replied. "I didn't get my wish!"

"What did you wish for?" Pat said.

Dennis looked mournful. "I wished that Einstein wouldn't tell any more stupid jokes!"

From: Einstein Anderson
To: Science Geeks
Experiment: Shine On—Using Bounced Light

I don't know about you, but even though I get the idea that the moon has phases because its light is reflected back at us from the sun, sometimes I get confused about how it actually works. Let's clear it up! Look at this diagram:

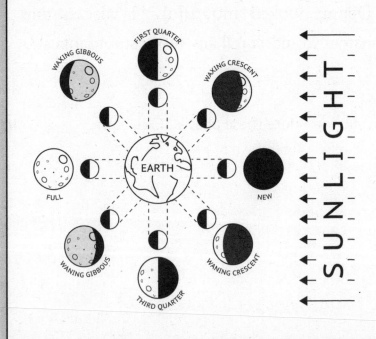

Notice that the sunlight is coming from the right side, the moon is always lit up on the side facing the sun, and exactly half of the moon is always bright. What changes is what we see, looking at the moon from the earth. The earth is in the center of this diagram and the dotted lines show what a person on that part of the earth would see when they look at the moon. Sometimes you see part bright and part dark, but when the moon is all dark, it's invisible. Got it? Great! You might want to try with some friends to make a kid-sized model like this. Have someone hold a flashlight (they are the sun), have another person stand in the center (they are the earth), and have someone walk around the earth with a ball to represent the moon. Can you reproduce these phases? Excellent!

Now, we all know that things that produce light like lamps and flashlights and torches are useful, but what about things that use reflected light? Let's make a cool spying device that uses reflected light to let you see around corners!

Here is what you need:

- A long box, like a shoebox
- Two small mirrors
- Tape
- Scissors

Open the box and tape the mirrors into the corners as shown in the drawing. It doesn't matter if the two mirrors are not the same size—a handle could stick out through the side of the box, but you must make sure the mirrors are both at a 45-degree angle. To test that, measure from the corner of the box to the place where the mirror is taped to the box. The other side of the mirror should be taped at exactly the same distance from the corner. If it is, it will be at a 45° angle (the little circle means "degree"). Then cut two holes in the side of the box opposite the mirrors. Put the lid back on and tape the box shut. Now when you look in the hole at the bottom you will see what the mirror in the top is seeing. This is handy if you want to look over a tall fence or around a corner without being seen.

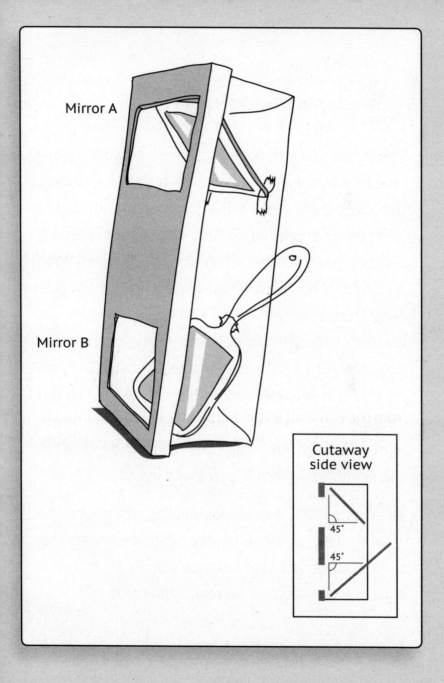

Mirror A

Mirror B

Cutaway side view

45°

45°

The Science Solution

The device you just made is called a periscope, and in the real world, submarines use this technology to peek out above the water. It's useful anywhere you need to look over or around an obstacle without being seen. It turns out that mirrors, which work by reflected light, are pretty handy, aren't they? Like a ball, light bounces away from an object it hits. And if the object is hard and smooth and shiny like a mirror (or even a store window) the light sends back images of things that are reflected. In your periscope, light comes into the top opening and reflects the image of what is there on the mirror. That light and image then bounces down to the bottom mirror, where it is reflected out to your eyes.

Could you make a really looooooong periscope? The answer is yes, but the longer the periscope, the smaller the image you would see. Big periscopes use magnifying lenses between the mirrors. Happy spying!

Lost in the Swamp

Every May, Sparta Middle School had a weekend trip to Carter Lake State Park. The sixth graders were usually the most excited because it was their first overnight school trip. Einstein's class was no different. On Friday morning everyone arrived early, carrying sleeping bags and overnight packs or gym bags.

Of course, Einstein had been to Carter Lake

many times with his family, and so had Paloma. Her Aunt Camilla had a house on a hill that looked over the lake. But this was different. The middle school kids all stayed in cabins on the other side of the lake. They would spend the weekend hiking, swimming, having a cook-out, and playing sports.

Einstein was in the same cabin as Pat, Jamal, and Stanley. They got up Saturday morning, ready for fun. Even Stanley seemed to be get-ting in the spirit. They'd been there twelve whole hours and he hadn't yet brought up a get-rich-quick scheme. He did complain a few times about not being able to bring along a phone, computer, or any other way of getting on the Internet.

"How am I going to stay up with the latest tech news?" he whined as they were getting dressed for breakfast.

"You mean, how are we going to play Angry Birds?" Jamal teased him.

"That, too," Stanley agreed.

"I guess we're just going to have to enjoy nature the old-fashioned way," Einstein said as he stuffed his pajamas into his sleeping bag. "You know, without technology."

"How boring!" Stanley replied.

After breakfast, Ms. Taylor, the other teachers, and the parents who had come along gathered all the kids together.

"The first thing we're doing is a nature walk," Ms. Taylor announced. "There are several self-guided trails in the park that are marked. They're very easy to follow—as long as you stay on them, you can't get lost. The numbers on the maps are signs on the trails that give you information about the trees, plants, animals, and rock formations in the park."

The teachers handed out maps to everyone and the kids split up into groups of four. Naturally, Einstein and Paloma formed their own group and naturally Pat wanted to come along, although he still had trouble talking whenever he was around Paloma. Jamal made their fourth.

"Let's take the Big Loop Trail," Paloma said, pointing to a dotted line on the map.

"Let's take the Little Loop," Jamal replied. "It's littler."

"Come on," Einstein said. "The Big Loop is only three miles. We can do that and still be back in time for a swim before lunch."

Pat just nodded.

"The trail starts just over there," Paloma said, pointing to an opening in the trees near the cabins. "Come on."

She took off, and Pat fell in next to her.

Einstein and Jamal followed. Just as they got on the trail, they heard someone huffing and puffing behind them.

"Hey, guys, do you mind if I join your group?" Stanley called as he ran to catch them.

Einstein saw Paloma start to frown. Stanley wasn't her favorite person. But before she could say anything, Einstein waved to Stanley to catch up.

"Come on," he said. "But you have to keep up."

"Me?" Stanley wheezed as he stopped to catch his breath. "Sure. I'm the best hiker in sixth grade."

"Oh, just come on," Paloma laughed.

Soon they were all walking along, talking and enjoying themselves. After a few minutes, Einstein spotted a large bird making lazy circles in the blue sky. He pointed out that its broad wings and short, fan-shaped tail meant that it was a hawk.

"I've got binoculars," Paloma said as she dug into the backpack she took everywhere. "Here." She handed the binoculars to Einstein.

"It's a red-tail," he said, and handed the binoculars to Jamal. "I wonder if we can spot its nest."

"What kind of nest does it make?" asked Pat.

"They usually build a nest of sticks high up in a tree or on a ledge," Einstein told him.

"I wonder what they eat," said Jamal as they started walking again.

"Small animals," Paloma told him. "Mostly small birds, and also small rodents like mice. They're raptors. That means they knock their prey down with their claws."

"Hey, that reminds me," Einstein said.

Everyone groaned and got ready for one of his silly jokes. Einstein was already laughing.

"How can you get a pet bird for hardly any money?" he said with a chuckle. "You plant bird seed!"

"That was for the birds!" said Jamal.

"Let's hurry," Stanley interrupted. "All this talk about food is making me hungry."

The trail started climbing, and soon they were in a clearing at the top of a hill. They could look down and see the lake and the cabins where they had started.

"That's south of here," Paloma said as she turned her map around. She held it up so Pat could look over her shoulder. "I think we're going north, then east, then south again."

"Uh, yeah," Pat agreed. "North."

"Maybe we should turn back," Stanley said. "I think it's almost time for lunch."

"No, it can't be much past ten," Einstein told him.

"How do you know what time it is, *Einstein*?" Stanley replied grumpily. "You're not wearing a watch and we don't have our phones with us."

"I can tell by how long the shadows are," Einstein replied, pointing to shadows of some nearby pine trees. "And by where the sun is in the sky. You can tell a lot just by looking at those two things. Since we have a map I know about where we are. And we can see the cabins from here, so I know which direction is south. At noon the sun will be at its highest point of the day and directly south, just over the cabins. But it's not."

"Yeah, I could have told you that," Stanley grumbled.

"Anyway, I have a watch," Jamal said. "And

Einstein is right. It's a little after ten. So keep walking, Stanley."

They all kept walking, following the trail as it left the top of the hill. After about ten minutes they were in a low swampy area, where the trees spread out.

"It must have rained recently," Paloma said, looking at the ground. "See how muddy it is? But which way does the trail go? I don't see any markers."

Einstein looked around. Paloma was right. There was no clear trail here and he couldn't see any markers on the trees.

"Hold on," he said. "Let's figure out where we should go."

"Oh, you always want to be in charge," Stanley complained. "Anyone can see the trail goes over by those rocks."

"I don't think so," said Einstein. "I think it goes over that little creek."

"Uh-uh," Stanley said. "I'm not getting my feet wet. The trail is this way."

With that he took off toward the rocks.

"Stanley, wait a minute!" Einstein called.

"You can wait if you want, *Einstein*," Stanley shouted over his shoulder. "I'm going to go get lunch!"

Stanley disappeared behind the boulders.

"We'd better get him," Paloma said.

Pat nodded. "You're right!" he said, and they both took off, trotting after Stanley. Jamal followed them.

"Well, I guess we'd better stay together," Einstein muttered, and he followed his friends.

Einstein caught up with the rest of his friends on the other side of the boulders, but there was no sign of Stanley. Then they heard him calling from the distance.

"Over here!" he shouted. "I found the trail. Follow my voice."

They did as he said, following his shouts through a stand of trees and then around another bunch of rocks. There was Stanley, resting on a large boulder.

"Okay," Paloma said, "Where's the trail?"

"Right there," Stanley said, pointing to a spot in the woods a few yards away. Pat went over to see.

"This is no trail," he said. "It's just a bare spot on the ground."

"Well, it looked like a trail," Stanley whined. "My feet hurt."

"Now I think we're really lost," Paloma said, squinting at the map in her hand. "Which way did we come?"

"I think it's that way," Jamal said, pointing in one direction.

"No, I think it's that way," Pat said, pointing in a different direction.

They all looked around uneasily. They could see only a short distance through the dense woods in any direction. There were no trails and no markings.

"We're all turned around," said Paloma. She sounded a little worried.

"We're lost!" Stanley cried. "I knew I should never have come with you!"

"Stay calm," Einstein told him. "The trail can't be far."

"But which way?" asked Paloma. "If we set off in the wrong direction, we'll only get more lost. We could wander around in circles without knowing it."

"We're lost!" Stanley cried again.

Einstein took the map from Paloma.

"We know the cabins are south of here," he said. "I think we're in this swampy area, so the trail is probably south of here, too."

"Lost in the swamp," Stanley moaned. "That's the end of my career."

"Relax," Einstein said, trying to sound confident. "All we have to do is figure out which way is south. Does anyone have a compass?"

Pat and Jamal shook their heads. "Paloma, you must have one in your backpack."

But Paloma shook her head, too. "No," she said. "I've been using the compass app on my phone. But I left my phone at home."

"Lost in the swamp!" Stanley moaned, even louder. "I'll never be a billionaire now."

"Jamal," Einstein asked, "What kind of watch do you have? Is it digital or does it have hands?"

"It has hands, but what difference does that make?" Jamal asked. He looked at his wrist. "It's ten forty-five. How does that help?"

"I don't want your watch to tell me the time," Einstein said. "I want it to show us how to get out of here."

Can you solve the mystery? How can Jamal's watch help Einstein find the way back?

"**Okay**, this I gotta see," Jamal said. "Here's my watch."

Einstein took the watch and held it flat. He looked up and found the sun shining between the treetops. He turned the watch so that the smaller hour hand pointed in the direction of the sun. He pushed back his glasses and thought for a minute. "That direction is south," he said, pointing. "Let's go."

He started walking in that direction with Paloma and Pat following.

"What do you mean, 'Let's go'?" Stanley protested, from his seat on the rock. "Why should we believe you?"

"You can stay if you want," Jamal told him. "But I'm following Einstein."

"Hey, wait up!" Stanley called, and ran after them.

With the group following him, Einstein walked carefully in the same direction, through a stand of trees and over a muddy creek. Then he cried out.

"Look! A trail marker!"

Sure enough, it was the marker for the Big Loop Trail.

"Einstein, how did you do that?" Pat asked as they started walking along the trail.

"It's like I said up on the hill," Einstein replied. "We know that the sun is due south at noon. Suppose we point the hour hand of a watch at the sun at that time. Then both the hands and the number twelve will point south.

Before noon, the sun is left of the number twelve, and after noon the sun is to the right."

"Okay, I think I see," Pat said.

"Once you have the hour hand pointed at the sun, you find the halfway point between that and the number twelve on the dial. That's south."

"Pretty cool," said Jamal. "I never realized that my watch could tell me compass directions."

"Hey, that's a great idea for an invention," said Stanley. "Nobody steal it!"

"Here you go," Einstein said to Jamal, handing him his watch as they walked along. Then he added, very seriously. "Don't lose it, or we won't be able to go swimming."

"Why not?" asked Jamal.

"Because then we won't have the time," Einstein said, laughing loudly at his own joke.

From: Einstein Anderson
To: Science Geeks
Experiment: Get Lost!

Lost. An idea so scary it lasted for 121 episodes on TV. Everyone gets lost sometime and it's good to know how to figure out where you are—or at least what direction to go in order to get back home. If you are lost in a city or town, you can ask someone for directions, and most cell phones have GPS (and a free compass app) that can locate you very precisely. But what if you are on a hike like Pat and Paloma and Stanley and I were, and your phone is out of juice, or back at home? Here are three different ways you can turn ordinary objects into a compass.

Here is what you need:
• An analog watch (one with hands)
• A piece of paper
• A pen or pencil
• A cup
• Some water
• A steel needle

- A strong stick about one yard (1m) long
- String
- 3 rocks

Method #1: This is the method I used when Stanley got us lost. Take your analog watch and hold it flat in your hand, then point the hour hand (the small one) toward the sun. Draw a line halfway between the hour hand and the 12. The side toward the sun points south, and the opposite direction is due north. If you don't have an analog watch, only a digital one, you can still do this. Check the time on your digital watch, draw a clock face on the paper with the hands where they would be on an analog watch, point the drawn hour hand toward the sun, and split the distance between that hand and the 12 to find the north/south line.

By the way, this only works in the northern hemisphere. If you are in the southern hemisphere, the north and south are reversed (north is toward the sun). Also, if your watch is on daylight savings time in the summer, you need to measure between the hour hand and 1:00, instead of 12:00. You still divide the distance in two because your watch hands go around twice in a day.

Got it? Great!

Method #2: This would be fun to try at home or at school, even if you're not lost.

Put a straight stick about 1 meter long (3 feet) upright in the ground at a level place with as much sunlight as possible. Put a stone at the end of the shadow it casts. Wait about 20 minutes and measure again. Put another marking stone at the end of the second shadow. Draw a straight line between the two stones.

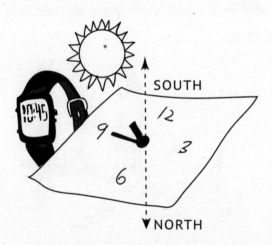

Stand with your left foot near the first mark and your right foot near the second mark. You will be facing north.

Method #3: Fill a cup 2/3 full of water. Carefully slide a needle into the water so that it floats on the surface tension on the top. Put the cup on a stable surface or hold it very still. If the needle is made of magnetic material it will act like a compass and turn itself to float in a north/south direction. The only catch is that you don't know which way is north and which is south. In the northern hemisphere, the sun is due south at noon, so you can estimate which way is south by figuring how far you are from noon and where the sun will be—or was—at 12:00.

The Science Solution

The floating needle is actually a compass—the north pole of the compass will always point to the north pole of earth if it is free to move—but the other methods of orienteering we used depend upon our knowledge of the rotation of the earth and its movement around the sun. We know that the sun rises in the east and sets in the west. That's because the earth rotates from west toward the east so the eastern horizon sees the sun first in the day and the west sees it last. At the middle of the day, noontime, the sun is directly to our south if we are in the northern hemisphere (to the north if you are in the southern hemisphere).

That's why the watch works as a compass. The position of the sun changes throughout the day, but at noon it will be due south. If you are lost in the morning, the north/south line will cross a point to the left of the 12, and in the afternoon it will cross a point to the right.

The trick with the stick uses the same clues provided by the earth's rotation, but it gives an east/west line instead of a north/south line. When you measure the shadow cast by the stick and mark the end of it, you are measuring the angle of the sun as it strikes the stick and casts a shadow. Twenty minutes later, the earth's rotation will move the shadow, so the line between the first mark and the second will run from west to east. When you connect those two points, you have a line that runs approximately from west to east.

If you want a really accurate line, you need to wait all day (depending on the time of year). If you take your first measurement of the length of the shadow in the morning, the shadow will grow shorter and shorter until noontime when it will be almost gone, then it will gradually get longer again. When you take the morning measurement, use a sharp stone or a piece of chalk. Tie the stone or chalk at the end of a string tied to the stick, exactly the length of the shadow. Now, using the string to keep your diameter constant, trace a half-circle around the stick. When the shadow grows back to the exact same length in the afternoon, it will be at a spot on the half-circle line. If you draw a line between the morning spot and the afternoon spot, it will be exactly true west/east. You might try this on a playground with a stick and chalk. See your sun and earth in action!

Breaking Point

It was Saturday morning and Lake Carter was filled with the yelling, splashing, and very happy kids from Sparta Middle School. This was one of the best parts of the annual school trip, the chance to relax and just have fun.

Einstein Anderson and his friends were right in the middle of it. After getting lost for a few minutes during their nature hike, they made it back in plenty of time for the morning swim. They all quickly changed into their swimsuits and ran into the water with the rest of the school.

"Let's race to the raft!" Paloma shouted, and dove into the water.

Pat dove in after her. Einstein and Jamal followed, with Stanley bringing up the rear. Pat was on the swim team, and he had no trouble catching up with Paloma, but for some reason, he just couldn't manage to pass her. Jamal churned past both of them and soon heaved himself out of the water on the raft.

Einstein didn't bother to try to beat any of them, but he was a good swimmer, so it didn't take long for him to reach the raft also. The four of them sat in the edge with their feet in the water and called out to Stanley who was paddling as hard as he could but was only half way.

"Come on, Stanley!" Pat shouted, like he was at a swim meet. Jamal whistled and even Paloma clapped to encourage him. Finally, he was close enough to grab hold of the wooden planks of the raft. He pulled himself around so he could use the ladder to climb up.

"Good race!" he panted. "I usually swim faster, but I must be weak from hunger."

The others laughed and even Stanley had to smile at his own boasting. After a moment Pat stood up and dove in the water. He was also an excellent diver. He swam back and hauled himself on the raft again. Then they started taking turns diving and swimming back.

"Hey, be careful!" Paloma warned after she had taken her dive. "One of the boards is broken."

Einstein saw the board she was talking about. He had to squint because he wasn't wearing his glasses. The board had cracked in half, but not all the way through.

"Someone must have jumped up and down," he said.

"My friend Susie can break boards with her hands," Paloma said, as she pulled herself out of the water.

"Yeah?" Jamal asked. "Like this?" He stood up and pretended to karate chop a board. "Hee-yah!" he shouted.

"Breaking boards is no big a deal," Stanley said. "Anyone can do it."

"Oh, come on, Stanley," Jamal protested. "Do you have to brag about *everything*?"

"Stanley's right," Einstein said, to Jamal's surprise. "Most people can learn to break boards pretty easily."

"Is it a trick?" Pat asked.

"Not a trick," Einstein answered. "It's physics."

Paloma nodded. "It's the speed of their hand that does it," she explained. "That's why karate teachers tell their students to imagine their hands going through the board, so they don't slow down at the last instant. Also, they hold the wood so you break with the grain, not against it. A karate student can learn to break boards pretty easily."

"See?" Stanley said to Jamal, indignantly. "I told you."

"One thing I always wondered," Pat said. "How come a baseball doesn't break when you hit it? I mean, you swing pretty fast, so why isn't it like the board?"

"Because the board is stiff," Paloma said, knocking the planks of the raft with her knuckles. "It bends a little, but not enough to absorb all the energy from the blow. Too much force and it will break. But the ball is elastic. It squishes down, then bounces away. If you see a stop-motion photo of a bat hitting a ball you can see the ball gets very squashed."

"Also, in karate, someone or something holds the board when it gets hit," Einstein added. "When you hit the ball, it's hanging in the air, so it absorbs the energy from the bat, then goes flying."

"Which reminds me . . ." Einstein began. Everyone else groaned and waited for the joke. Einstein was already laughing as he said,

"What's the best way to carve wood? Whittle by whittle!"

Paloma stood up. "That was really bad, *Einstein*," she said good-naturedly. "I'm going to swim back." And with that, she dove in.

A short time later they were all on the beach and looking for their towels. Einstein found his and also put on his glasses. As the world came back into focus he saw something he didn't want to see. It was Gary and Andrea, the two eighth graders who had been so angry when the sixth grade won the winter snow sculpture competition.

They couldn't have looked more different from each other. Gary was a tall, beefy blond kid with short hair, while Andrea was a tall, African American girl with a big mop of curly black hair. But Einstein had never seen them apart. He thought that maybe Gary and Andrea were best friends the way he and Paloma were best friends, but he never had the guts to ask.

Now the two of them were just a few feet away, near the dock that went out into the lake. They hadn't spotted Einstein yet and he wanted to keep it that way. They might be even angrier now, after Ms. Taylor's class beat them in the Spring Fair science competition.

The two of them were carrying fishing poles and were having some sort of disagreement.

"How can we cut the fishing line without a knife?" Gary was complaining as he bent over a small fishing tackle box. He held a spool of thin, nylon fishing line.

"I don't know," Andrea replied. "Why didn't you bring one?"

"Because I thought you were bringing one."

"Why did you think I was bringing one? I

thought you were bringing one. Why didn't you bring one?"

"Because I thought you were bringing one."

They kept at it like that. Then both Andrea and Gary looked up at the same time.

"Well, look who it is," Gary said, as he straightened up. "That little wise guy, Alfred Eisenstein."

Einstein started to correct him, but stopped himself just in time.

"What are you looking at, *Einstein*?" Andrea sneered. "You've never seen anyone go fishing before?"

"No, I go fishing all the time, with my dad," Einstein replied, trying to sound as friendly as possible.

"Oh, so I suppose you're an expert at *that*, too?" Andrea said.

"Uh, no," Einstein mumbled.

He felt a touch on his shoulder. He turned his head to the right and saw Pat standing next to him. Pat wasn't as big as Gary or Andrea, but he was tall, and he looked pretty confident.

"Hey, Einstein," he said, quietly. "What's going on?"

"What's going on is we've had enough of you little kids messing everything up," Gary said. He was starting to get red in the face. "And we're not letting you mess up this week-end, either."

"That's right," Andrea agreed, as she took a step toward Einstein and Pat. "We're not going to let you little babies get in our way. Starting right now: no sixth graders are al-lowed on the dock while we fish!"

"Hey, good rule!" Gary chuckled and he gave Andrea a fist bump.

"You can't do that!" Paloma had appeared at Einstein's left side, along with Jamal. "We'll tell the teachers."

"Go ahead and run to the teachers," Andrea taunted Paloma. "We said you sixth graders are all big babies."

"We don't need the teachers," Einstein said, as calmly as he could. Everyone stopped and looked at him. Even Gary and Andrea looked surprised. "I just mean, I know a way we can settle this," Einstein told them, then quickly added, "using science."

"Oh, some more of that science stuff," Gary said. "What are you going to do? Build a time machine and send us back to the future?"

"Uh, no," Einstein replied. "I thought I would just help you."

"Help *me*?" Gary cried, getting even redder. "I don't need help from a stupid genius."

Einstein gave Paloma a look to make sure she didn't say there was no such thing as a "stupid genius." Then he continued.

"Uh, I just meant I can cut your fishing line for you," he said, pointing to the fishing tackle. "That's what you needed, right?"

Gary looked confused. "Uh, that's right, we did." Then he got angry again. "So you have scissors, so what? We can get our own scissors."

"I told you to bring one," Andrea said.

"No, you didn't."

"Yes, I did!"

Einstein cleared his throat.

"Uh, I didn't mean I would use scissors. I

meant I would cut the fishing line with my bare hands."

Gary laughed. "Oh, that's no big deal. I can do that."

"Okay," Einstein said. "Let's have a contest. I bet you can't break the line with your hands, but I can. If I win, you leave the sixth graders alone."

"And if I win?" Gary asked, suspiciously.

"If you win," Paloma said quickly, "we tell the whole school that you're a bigger genius than Einstein."

"Plus, the sixth graders don't get to use the dock," Andrea added.

"It's a bet!" Einstein declared.

"Einstein, are you sure?" Pat whispered to him. "If you lose, the whole sixth grade is going to be mighty unhappy."

"Don't worry," Einstein replied. "I'm sure I'm going to win."

Can you solve the mystery? How can Einstein be so sure he will win the bet?

"**I know,**" Jamal said quietly, so Gary couldn't hear. "You're going to karate chop it."

"No," Einstein told him with a smile. "Don't ever try that—you'll just wind up cutting your hand."

"Then how?" Jamal asked.

Einstein just shrugged as if to say, "You'll see."

Gary had grabbed a length of the fishing line.

"Now remember," Einstein said. "You can only use your bare hands."

Gary wrapped the line around one hand, then the other. Then he tried to pull his hands apart and break the line that way.

"Ow!" he grunted and quickly stopped. "That hurts!"

"You big baby," Andrea scolded him.

"It was cutting me," Gary complained and he showed her the red marks on the backs of his hands.

"You can't break it that way. It has way too much tensile strength," Einstein said. Then he added. "That means it can hold a lot of weight before it snaps."

"Oh, yeah?" Gary said, angrily. "Then how are you going to break it?"

"By making the line break itself," Einstein replied. "Like this."

He took the spool of fishing line and carefully wrapped some around his hand and fingers. But he did it in a special way, making the line loop around itself. Then with a quick motion, he pulled the free end. The line broke with a snap.

Jamal, Pat, and Paloma cheered.

"How'd you do that?" Andrea asked, forgetting to be angry for a moment.

Einstein took the fishing line and slowly wrapped it around his hand the same way, showing Gary and Andrea what he did.

"The trick," he said, "is to loop the line against itself. That concentrates all your force on the tiny spot where the line crosses. The line itself acts like a knife blade. When you suddenly jerk your hands apart, the line cuts through itself instead of cutting into your hand."

"That's not fair!" Gary whined. "It's another science trick!" Then he quickly told Einstein, "Show me again."

Einstein did the trick another couple of times, very slowly so Gary and Andrea could see exactly how to wrap the line around their hands without getting hurt. Then they both did it.

"Hey! I'm Superman!" Gary cried, when his line snapped.

"Come on, let's go trick someone else," Andrea said, as she did it.

They both walked away, without another word to Einstein or his friends.

"Einstein's the Superman," Jamal said. "How'd you know how to do that?"

"I saw it on YouTube," Einstein replied. "It's just physics, knowing where and how to apply force."

Paloma laughed. "I don't know, Einstein," she said. "This time I think it was a little bit of magic. You made Gary and Andrea disappear."

They all laughed, then Einstein cleared his throat.

"Uh, that reminds me . . ." he began.

Jamal and Pat groaned in protest, but Paloma stopped them. "No, let him tell his joke. He earned it."

Einstein was already laughing. "Why is it easy to weigh a fish?"

"I don't know," Paloma said, cheerfully. "Why?"

"Because they all have scales!"

From: Einstein Anderson
To: Science Geeks
Experiment: String Break

Here is a really cool, really simple way that you can break string or fishing line. Amaze your friends!

Here is what you need:

• String or fishing line
• Your two hands

First, wrap the string around your left hand a couple of times, and then wrap it around your right hand. This is the way most people try to break string. The harder you pull, the more you hurt your hands!

Now, wrap the string once around your left hand. Be sure to leave a tail about 8 inches (20 cm) long, before you start the wrap. This time, when you start the second wrap around your hand, turn your hand over so that there is a twist in the string (see the picture below). Pull sharply on the end of the string so that it pulls against itself, and presto! Your string will break!

This will work every time, except with very thick string or fishing line. It works because when the string crosses over itself, the two pieces of string meet at a very narrow, precise point and all the pressure of your pull is concentrated at that exact point. This reduces the tensile strength of the string or line to about 20% of what it was without the wrap. Snap! You can break it right off!

Give yourself a break today!

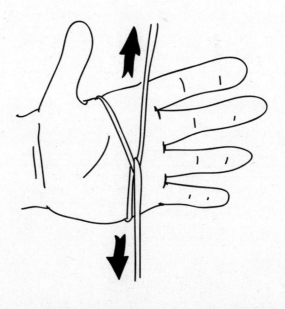